W9-AHY-107

On Eagle Cove

By Jane Yolen

Pictures by Elizabeth Dulemba

The**Cornell**Lab Publishing Group

Design by Shan Stumpf, Brian Scott Sockin,
and Jill Leichter

ISBN: 978-1-943645-48-0

10 9 8 7 6 5 4 3 2 1

Published by:
The Cornell Lab Publishing Group
An imprint of WunderMill, Inc.
321 Glen Echo Lane, Ste. C
Cary, NC 27518
www.cornelllabpg.com

www.wundermillbooks.com

Back matter photos: Bald Eagle standing on a rock, ©Darren Clark/Macaulay
Library; blackbird chasing eagle, ©Margaret F. Viens/Macaulay Library;
two eagles on a branch, ©Glenn Lahde/Macaulay Library; soaring eagle
©Cory Kampf/Macaulay Library; all other photos, ©Shutterstock.

Jane: For David, who showed me my first eagle.
Elizabeth: To Stan, always...

As I walked out towards Eagle Cove,
Wandering through a greening grove,

I saw just where the pathway led—
And spied a great big lake ahead.
Tall trees shook fists at bluest sky
Just as a giant bird soared by.

Above, an even bigger flew,
And that was when I truly knew—

Eagles.
Two.

I signaled Mom so she could spy
The eagles flying in the sky.

At first I thought
it was a fight.

They grasped each others' talons tight,

Cartwheeling all
across the sky,

Then broke apart,
and back did fly.

They chased each other
to and fro,

Then parted —
quite an aerial show.

One with talons taut, to fish
And then to share that new caught dish.
The other off to a mammoth tree.
And on that tree, what did I see?

A massive, messy, giant nest.
And that was when I truly guessed:
A mating pair!

You know the rest:
The nest was made of sticks, moss, grass,
Interwoven, sure to last.

But quite soon after, off they flew.
Where they went next, I never knew.

But two months later, we went back
To their giant nesting shack.

We climbed a big hill, found a cliff,
Both sat down and wondered if
We'd see into the eagles' nest.

And there they were
—a perfect guess!

We saw a duo of large chicks
Avoiding all the pointed sticks.

Each chick was half their parents' size,
With fuzzy feathers, great big eyes.

They couldn't yet leave penthouse aerie.
(The drop alone looked steep and scary.)
But Mom said soon enough they'd fly
On eagle wings across the sky.

I knew they'd cartwheel like the rest,
Then find a mate, build a big nest.

Knew year by year, that nest would grow,
Shading everything below:
The limb, the bark, the roots of tree,
And standing there beneath, us three,

In a lovely greening grove,
As we walked home from Eagle Cove.

Learn more about the
BALD EAGLE

Bald Eagles are one of the largest birds in North America. They live a long time for a bird—the oldest Bald Eagle lived to be 38 years old. Their favorite food is fish, and they eat lots of them. From high up in the sky, they can see a fish under the water. Then they swoop down and grab it by just getting their feet a little wet. They also eat small animals, ducks, and even snakes.

Their eyes are the same size as ours, but they see a lot better than we do, and can see colors we can't see. We call people with excellent vision "eagle-eyed," but eagles have much sharper vision than we do. Imagine being able to spot a rabbit from three miles away!

The Bald Eagle's pointed beak is perfect for ripping through the scales of a fish or the skin of an animal.

You might see a Bald Eagle every day and not even know it. Just search the back of a dollar bill for the official seal of the United States, designed in 1782.

Bald Eagles have a habit of stealing their meals from other animals. Even so, sometimes smaller birds will chase the eagle away, like this Red-winged Blackbird.

Have you ever seen a Bald Eagle's nest? Start by looking near water, and then look up high—eagles like to have a good view. The nest usually sits at the top of a tall tree and looks like a large, deep basket.

It can take a pair of eagles as long as three months to build a nest that is six feet across and four feet deep. Their hard work won't go to waste—once they build it, Bald Eagles will often return to the same nest year after year. They use sticks, small branches, grass, and moss to make the nest, and line the inside with soft lichen and downy feathers.

The largest bird nest in the world was built by a pair of Bald Eagles in Florida. It was more than nine feet wide and 20 feet tall, and it weighed more than two tons!

The Bald Eagle's large, curved claws are just right for grabbing a meal, whether it is fish from the water, or an animal on land.

A Bald Eagle watches over two downy chicks in a huge treetop nest.

A young Bald Eagle tests her wings. She looks different than her parents. It will take four years for her to become an adult with a bright white head and yellow beak.

make their flying muscles strong. They might even take small practice flights by hopping onto a nearby branch with their wings stretched.

When they are four or five years old, Bald Eagles start looking for a mate. One way a pair of eagles may get to know each other is to show off their skills with a special dance in the air. High up in the sky together, they swoop, cartwheel, and then lock their talons and tumble back to earth, only to break away and fly up moments before they hit the ground.

Sadly, we did not always protect and treasure Bald Eagles. When they came into contact with humans, they had a hard time and came close to disappearing entirely.

Bald Eagles lay their eggs early in the spring, and both parents take turns keeping them warm. When they hatch, young eagles look like gray, wobbly, puff balls with big eyes and a large beak. In a few weeks, they get better at staying warm on their own, and soon they start to grow flight feathers. After a couple months, the young eagles get ready to leave the nest.

While they are growing, they eat lots of small animals and fish that their parents bring to them on the nest. When they poop, they aim out over the edge of their nest, so the nest stays nice and clean.

Once young Bald Eagles grow flight feathers, they test their wings by hopping up and down on the nest and flapping them over and over. This will

The**Cornell**Lab Publishing Group

The Cornell Lab of Ornithology is a world leader in the study, appreciation, and conservation of birds. As with all Cornell Lab Publishing Group books, 35% of the net proceeds from the sale of *On Eagle Cove* will directly support the Cornell Lab's projects, such as children's educational and community programs.

For hundreds of years, the birds were hunted because people thought they killed too many farm animals or ate too much fish. More recently, they were poisoned by a pesticide, DDT, which weakened their eggshells so much that their eggs would crumble before their chicks could hatch.

When DDT was banned in 1972, Bald Eagle eggs slowly grew strong again. Soon after, Bald Eagles became protected under the Endangered Species Act, and could no longer be killed without breaking the law.

Today, their numbers have increased so much, it is not that unusual to see a Bald Eagle soaring overhead. Even though they are no longer listed on the Endangered Species List, we still have special laws that protect them and other birds.

The next time you are near a lake or a river, look way up in the trees and see if you can spot a large bundle of sticks in the shape of a basket. Keep your eye out when you are fishing from a boat—an eagle might swoop down and steal your catch. Look closely at large birds soaring overhead, and see if you can spot the adult Bald Eagle's bright white head. Once you see a Bald Eagle in the wild, you will never forget it!

Bald Eagles mate for life. They build their nests together, and take turns finding food for their young and keeping their eggs and chicks warm when the weather is cold.

When Bald Eagles soar, their wings measure seven feet from tip to tip. Despite being so large, they are skilled fliers.